HIGGLETY PIGGLETY POP!
OR
THERE MUST BE MORE TO LIFE

HIGGLETY PIGGLETY POP!

 OR

THERE MUST BE MORE TO LIFE

STORY AND PICTURES BY

MAURICE SENDAK

HARPER & ROW, PUBLISHERS · ESTABLISHED 1817

SEN   999

FOR JENNIE

HIGGLETY PIGGLETY POP!
OR
THERE MUST BE MORE TO LIFE

Chapter 1

Once Jennie had everything. She slept on a round pillow upstairs and a square pillow downstairs. She had her own comb and brush, two different bottles of pills, eyedrops, eardrops, a thermometer, and for cold weather a red wool sweater. There were two windows for her to look out of and two bowls to eat from. She even had a master who loved her.

But Jennie didn't care. In the middle of the night she packed everything in a black leather bag with gold buckles and looked out of her favorite window for the last time.

"You have everything," said the potted plant that happened to be looking out the same window.

Jennie nibbled a leaf.

"You have two windows," said the plant. "I have only one."

Jennie sighed and bit off another leaf. The plant continued. "Two pillows, two bowls, a red wool sweater, eyedrops, eardrops, two different bottles of pills, a thermometer, and he even loves you."

"That is true," said Jennie, chewing more leaves.

"You have everything," repeated the plant.

Jennie only nodded, her mouth full of leaves.

"Then why are you leaving?"

"Because," said Jennie, snapping off the stem and blossom, "I am discontented. I want something I do not have. There must be more to life than having everything!"

The plant had nothing to say.

It had nothing left to say it with.

Chapter 2

Jennie took everything and went out into the world. On the corner she met a small pig wearing large sandwich boards. He smiled and pointed to a box attached to the front board on which was printed: *Free Sandwiches, Please Take.* Jennie chose a tuna on rye and gobbled it as she read the advertisement on the board.

It said: *Looking for Something Different?*

"Yes!" shouted Jennie, reaching for a ham, Swiss cheese and Russian dressing on pumpernickel. She continued to read: *Wanted! Leading Lady for The World Mother Goose Theatre! Plenty to Eat!* (The pig turned around.) *If You Have Experience, Call* EX *1–1212.*

As loud as she could, Jennie called, "EX 1–1212!"

The pig turned around again. "You called?"

"Yes. I want to be the leading lady for The World Mother Goose Theatre." She took an anchovy, tomato and egg on toast.

"I'm happy to hear it," said the pig. "Have you——"

"I have everything," interrupted Jennie, wiping egg off her beard and pointing to the black leather bag with gold buckles.

"Experience too?"

Jennie sniffed a liverwurst and onion on white bread. "Never heard of it."

The small pig shook his head sadly. "To be leading lady of The World Mother Goose Theatre you must have experience."

"How much time do I have to get it?" asked Jennie, carefully picking the lettuce out of a turkey, bacon and mayonnaise sandwich.

"By the first night of the full moon." They both looked up at the sky. The moon was nearly full.

"I'll never make it," said Jennie.

"If you do," said the small pig, "don't call us, we'll call you," and he vanished so quickly Jennie just had time to snatch the last sandwich. It was salami. Her favorite.

Chapter 3

It was dawn and a horse pulling a milk wagon clip-clopped down the pale street.

The milkman stopped to offer Jennie a ride. He stared at her black leather bag with gold buckles and said, "You must be going to a very terrific place."

"Of course," said Jennie, licking her paw.

"The most terrific place on my route is the big white house outside of town."

Jennie yawned. "That's just where I'm going."

"I thought so," said the milkman, pleased with himself.

"You think fast," sniffed Jennie, "for a cat."

The milkman laughed and winked slyly. "I've even guessed that you're the new nurse for Baby."

"You *are* sharp," said Jennie, wagging her tail. "But can you guess what it's like to miss breakfast?"

"Help yourself," said the milkman.

Jennie thanked him and climbed to the back of the wagon. She stuck her nose into a raspberry yogurt, and before the wagon reached the corner she had swallowed a whole farmer cheese and licked a pint bottle of milk clean.

"You're the seventh nurse Baby's had," said the milkman. "All the others failed."

Jennie sucked the insides out of half a dozen brown eggs. "How did they fail?"

"They couldn't make Baby eat."

"Imagine not wanting to eat," murmured Jennie, sampling the skimmed milk. "What happened to the other six nurses?"

"They just disappeared. Some say," the milkman whispered, "they were fed to the lion locked up in the cellar of the big white house. How do you like that?"

13

"Awful!" coughed Jennie, and she deliberately knocked over the bottle of skimmed milk. "But I won't fail. I'll make Baby eat."

"*That* will be an experience!" the milkman shouted.

"How wonderful," sighed Jennie as she licked a stick of butter. "That's just what I need."

They came to the edge of town and the road turned bumpy. The wagon creaked, the bottles clinked; and over a hill and past some trees the big white house appeared.

Jennie took her black leather bag with gold buckles, jumped down, and said, "Thank you very much."

"You're welcome," said the milkman. "And I wish you luck with Baby."

"I wish you luck with your future deliveries," answered Jennie, and she ran up to the front door and pulled the bell.

The milkman had nothing to say.

There was nothing left to deliver.

Chapter 4

The parlormaid opened the front door and said, "You must be Baby's new nurse."

"I'm certainly not nurse's new baby," snapped Jennie, proud of her quick repartee.

"Follow me," said the parlormaid. She showed Jennie into a fine-smelling room—the kitchen.

"This house has everything," said Jennie.

The parlormaid shook her head. "Everything but a good nurse for Baby." She covered a tray and put it to one side. "Baby's breakfast," she explained.

Jennie fainted.

"Heavens!" cried the parlormaid. She promptly filled a pan with water and dumped it over Jennie's head.

Jennie was moaning. "Pancakes . . . buttermilk pancakes."

The parlormaid frantically mixed some batter and put it up to fry. She popped the first pancake into Jennie's drooping mouth. "What's the matter with you?"

"The doctors call it jumping stomach," she groaned. "Any sugar?"

The parlormaid knocked boxes and jars onto the floor, looking for the sugar. Jennie pointed wearily to the top shelf. "Over there, next to the syrup. Syrup helps too."

The parlormaid fed Jennie the dripping pancakes. "Jumping stomach sounds serious," she sighed, mopping her brow with sticky fingers. "I hope it doesn't happen often."

"I never faint on the job," said Jennie. "You don't have to worry. I'll make Baby eat."

"Don't be too confident. You just get one chance and if you fail, the downstairs lion eats you up. *That's* an experience you won't soon forget!"

Jennie's stomach really jumped. "One experience is enough for me," she said. "Any coffee?"

The parlormaid put a pot of coffee on the stove.

Jennie was licking syrup off her nose. "Doesn't Baby have a name?"

"She used to, but everyone's forgotten what it is."

"Even her mother and father?" asked Jennie. She sniffed. "Coffee's ready."

"Of course not," laughed the parlormaid as she poured Jennie a cup. "But they've been away ever so long. I must remember to ask them when they get back."

Jennie lapped her coffee daintily. "Where are they?"

"Oh," said the parlormaid, waving her arm, "at the Castle Yonder." Before Jennie could ask where that was, a bell rang.

"Baby calling," said the parlormaid, reaching for the breakfast tray. "Follow me."

She led Jennie down a long hallway lit on either side by tall yellow windows. They looked buttery in the morning light.

"What's your name?" asked Jennie.

"Rhoda. May I ask what you have in your black leather bag with gold buckles?"

"Everything." They were climbing a narrow staircase. Rhoda stopped to look when Jennie opened her bag.

"You *do* have everything."

"I have even more," Jennie said modestly. "Two windows that I left at home."

"I repeat, you *do* have everything."

"You can say that again." But before Rhoda could decide whether or not she would, they reached the nursery.

Chapter 5

"Baby, here is Nurse." Rhoda uncovered the tray and put it on the table.

"NO EAT!" said Baby.

Jennie smelled orange juice, oatmeal, soft-boiled egg, and vanilla pudding.

"Good luck," whispered Rhoda, "and don't forget, only one chance."

"I'll make the most of it," said Jennie, nosing her way toward Baby's breakfast. Rhoda quietly closed the door behind her.

Jennie sipped the orange juice. "Yum, yum."

"NO YUM!" shouted Baby.

"You needn't shout!" Jennie choked, spilling orange juice all over her beard. "I'm not deaf."

"SHOUT!" shouted Baby.

Jennie wiped her beard on the rug. "If you do not eat, you will not grow."

"NO EAT! NO GROW! SHOUT!"

Jennie sighed and neatly tapped the top off the soft-boiled egg. "Baby want a bite?"

"NO BITE!"

"GOOD!" snapped Jennie, and she gulped the egg, shell and all.

Breakfast was disappearing into Nurse, and suddenly Baby wanted some too. "EAT!" she cried, pointing to the cereal.

Jennie thanked Baby and gobbled up the oatmeal.

"NO EAT!" Baby screamed. She caught hold of Jennie's tail and bit hard. Jennie howled and twisted around. They sat staring at each other, growling and showing their teeth.

"My tail isn't breakfast," snarled Jennie. "Why didn't you say you were hungry? Here's some vanilla pudding."

Baby tried to get at it first and it fell on the floor.

"Greedy!" yapped Jennie as she pounced on the pudding.

Baby rolled over Jennie and when they came right side up, the pudding was gone.

Jennie whimpered. "I've failed my experience! I didn't mean to eat the pudding. I *hate* vanilla pudding!"

A terrible roar shook the floor under her feet.

"LION EAT!" shouted Baby as she scrambled toward the bell marked LION.

Jennie scooped Baby up, dropped her into the black leather bag with gold buckles, and sat down to think. Baby was kicking and punching and yowling inside the bag. Jennie heard her bowls smash, the thermometer snap, and the pillows rip. She chewed her paw, scratched her ear, and thought some more.

Baby's hand reached out of the bag, and the comb and brush went flying out the window.

Then Jennie remembered what Rhoda had told her.

She sniffed around for a telephone book and looked up Castle Yonder. The number was EX 1–1212. "That sounds familiar," thought Jennie.

A red wool sweater, partly unraveled, rolled out of the black leather bag. Jennie quickly dialed the number.

A lady's voice answered: "Hello there."

"Hello, this is Nurse and I'd like to speak to Baby's mother."

"Speaking. Oh, I'm so glad you called. You see, we moved to Castle Yonder, and what with hustling and bustling we forgot our old address and phone number and just didn't know how to get in touch."

"I don't know Hustling or Bustling," said Jennie, "but whoever they are, they made you forget Baby too."

"I know. We miss her so much. Could you send her back to us right away?"

Eyedrops, eardrops, and two different bottles of pills went smash against the wall.

"Of course," Jennie said eagerly. "She's already packed. I just have to put a stamp on and mail her."

"Oh, you mustn't do that. The postman never comes this way."

"Then how do I send her?"

"By lion," said the lady. "There is one in the cellar and he knows the way."

Jennie shivered. "Did you know that lion has eaten up six nurses and I don't know how many babies?"

"Tell him Baby's name and he won't dare eat her."

"What *is* Baby's name? And what about *me?*"

There was no answer.

"Hello? Hello?"

It was no use. The lady had hung up.

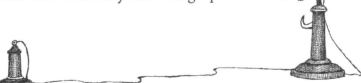

Chapter 6

Jennie left a note for Rhoda. It said: "I am personally taking Baby to Castle Yonder myself. Somebody will give me a lift. Yours sincerely, Nurse Jennie. P. S. I can't send her by lion. He would only eat her up along the way."

Jennie picked up her black leather bag with gold buckles, with Baby sleeping inside, and stepped lightly down the long hallway. The butter-yellow windows had darkened to bean-soup black, and she turned left instead of right.

Jennie had started down the wrong staircase.

Down she went and down some more, and the steps were narrow and slippery and never seemed to end. There was no sound but Baby snoring inside the black leather bag. The snore grew to a growl.

"Quiet in there."

"Lion eat," mumbled Baby in her sleep.

The growling turned to yowling, and Jennie was about to shake Baby up when she bumped her nose.

The staircase had come to an end at a wooden door. It creaked open and the lion roared, "Another nurse, and a fat one too!"

Jennie whimpered. "I can only stay a minute."

"Fine! That's all I need to eat a fat little dog."

"You must take Baby to Castle Yonder," Jennie yelped. "Her mother said so." She pushed the black leather bag an inch toward him and wagged her tail hopefully.

The lion sniffed the bag, closed his eyes, and sniffed again. "Ah, Baby. I haven't eaten a baby in such a long time."

Jennie's tail stiffened. "You're supposed to eat nurses," she snapped, "and I'm a nurse and I couldn't make Baby eat."

The lion laughed. "Well, if Baby won't eat, I'll eat Baby.

Besides," he snarled, "I really couldn't stomach another nurse." And he crept closer to the bag.

"You can't eat Baby. I'll tell you her name!"

The lion turned slowly, his eyes narrowed, spiteful and waiting.

Jennie twisted around frantically and gnawed her tail. "It's Mona!" she cried.

The lion sneered and began unbuckling the gold buckles with his teeth.

Jennie ran in circles, yapping. "Anna! Pearl! Natalie! Barbara!"

The lion grunted with pleasure, lifted the top of the bag, and opened his mouth wide.

Baby woke up, looked up, and flopped backward onto the stone floor. "NO EAT!" she screamed.

Jennie tore open the black leather bag and thrust it under the lion's nose. "Here! Take everything, but don't eat Baby."

The lion sniffed. "Broken bowls, half a thermometer, torn pillows. That is *nothing* and you can keep it!" He stretched his reeking jaws over Baby.

There was only one thing left to do. Jennie sighed and stuck her head into the lion's mouth. "Please eat me. I need the experience anyway. Otherwise The World Mother Goose Theatre might never——"

The lion's jaws snapped shut so fast Jennie barely had time to pull her head out. The tip of her beard remained inside and never grew back again.

"Would you say that again?" asked the lion.

Jennie was happy to oblige, now that his dreadful mouth was shut. The next instant the lion bent his shaggy head and picked up Baby by her nightdress.

"What are you *doing?*" barked Jennie. The lion stepped over her with Baby dangling from his jaws.

Jennie nipped helplessly at his heels. "Where are you taking

36

her?" The lion pressed a paw against one wall and a hidden door sprang open.

For a moment he crouched silently, then leaped high into the night.

"Wait! Don't eat Baby!" cried Jennie.

There was no answer.

Jennie looked up at the sky. The stars were shining. The moon was full.

Chapter 7

Now Jennie had nothing. There were no pillows to sleep on and no bowls to eat from. There was nowhere to sleep and nothing to eat. She wandered out into the night, dragging her black leather bag with gold buckles. The wind blew cold and Jennie sneezed. But there was no thermometer to check her temperature and no red wool sweater to cover herself along the way. There was no way to go.

Jennie's beard was tangled, her coat was in knots, and the comb and brush were lost. Her eyedrops, eardrops, and two different bottles of pills were spilt forever. She stretched out beneath an ash tree, her nose between her paws, and sighed.

"There must be more to life than having nothing."

"That's just what I was thinking," groaned the ash tree.

Jennie looked up. "I can't imagine why," she said. "You have everything."

The ash tree moaned and sprinkled her with leaves.

"You are taller than I am."

"Sixty feet taller, to be exact," muttered the ash, shedding more leaves.

"You have a place to live, a very broad top, friends all around, and surely someone loves you."

"Oh," fluttered the tree, "that is certainly true. I am the best-known and most desirable ash, anywhere."

"You have everything," said Jennie, circling in the fallen leaves for a comfortable position.

The ash tree nodded miserably, spilling leaves like yellow tears.

"Then why are you complaining?" asked Jennie, half buried by this time.

"Because," wailed the ash, letting fall a great shower of

leaves, "the winter is nearly here and I am discontented. The birds are gone, my leaves are dead, and I'll soon have nothing but the empty, frozen night."

Jennie had nothing to say. Leaves piled high above her, so she sighed and closed her eyes instead.

Chapter 8

Lions chased through Jennie's head. She caught one and was just about to bite when voices softly called: "Jennie." She growled and dreamt some more. The lion said, "Please eat me up, there's nothing more to life," when again the voices called. She kicked her legs and tried once more. The lion's head was in her mouth and: "Jennie."

The night hummed. Stars whirled in the full-moon sky and Jennie slowly shook away her leafy bed.

"Who's there?" she gruffed. "I'm just having dinner."

"Jennie."

Before her eyes an open place appeared. Sharply, as in a dream, she saw three figures standing, dark against the moon. They were clapping and calling her name.

Jennie didn't move. She barked and the echo scared her. She sniffed cautiously instead.

A familiar smell set her tail spinning and she ran, lumping and skittering, head over paws, across the open place. Jennie jumped from one figure to the other, licking their faces and dancing around their feet.

"Rhoda! Pig! Milkman!" She sniffed the free-sandwich box attached to the small pig's board. It was empty. "What are you all doing here?"

"We are actors in The World Mother Goose Theatre," said Rhoda.

The milkman bowed low. "And we've come to welcome our new leading lady."

Jennie sat up and begged. "Me?"

"You," they answered.

"Don't you remember?" said the small pig. "We promised to call when you had your experience."

"But I never did," Jennie sighed. "I never fed Baby and the lion never ate me."

"You stuck your head in the lion's mouth," said someone, from over the treetops. "*That* was an experience!"

At the sound of this voice, Rhoda, the pig, and the milkman disappeared into the darkness. Jennie looked up and saw the moon coming closer and closer. It was nearly on top of her when she saw it wasn't the moon at all. It was a lady, round on top, middle, and bottom, and dressed in shabby white.

"Don't you remember me?" the lady asked, stepping out of the night air.

Jennie whimpered nervously.

"NO EAT!" the lady shouted.

"Baby!" cried Jennie, flopping on her back. "How big and fat you've grown!"

"In the twinkling of an eye," she said as she knelt and scratched Jennie's stomach.

"You escaped from the lion!"

"Thanks to you. You guessed my name just in time."

Jennie shook her head. "That isn't so. All I said was The World Mother Goose——"

"There! You knew my name all the time." She was laughing.

Jennie ran yapping around in circles, scattering leaves. "The leading lady," she panted. "I'm the leading lady!"

"Yes, Jennie, and I have chosen a very special play for you, one to suit your very particular appetite." At the mention of appetite, Jennie's nose twitched.

"You are the leading lady in our new production of *Higglety Pigglety Pop!*"

"Higglety Pigglety Pop! How beautiful," Jennie sighed.

"I'm in it too!" cried Rhoda, who appeared suddenly in a captivating costume.

"And me," said the small pig, who was wearing a top hat and a pince-nez on his snout.

"And me," said the milkman, sporting a very gaudy uniform.

"And me!" roared the lion, pouncing from behind a tree, wearing nothing at all.

"Not me!" yelped Jennie, leaping into the lady's arms.

"You needn't worry," the lion grunted. "Only the leading lady gets to eat in *Higglety Pigglety Pop!*"

"Higglety Pigglety Pop! How beautiful." And Jennie sighed again.

Chimes, sharp as starlight, sounded from somewhere deep in the forest. It was time to begin.

They all climbed up on the lion's back.

"To the Castle Yonder!" the lady shouted and the lion sprang forward. He ran so fast the forest seemed to melt in moonshine and fade away altogether into the starry night.

But Jennie noticed nothing. She was too busy learning her part in *Higglety Pigglety Pop!*

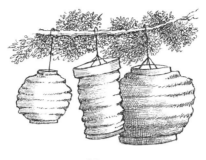

Chapter 9

It was time to begin. The stage was set in the park of the Castle Yonder. Colored lanterns, brightly lit, were strung from branches, and while the lion showed the audience to their seats a little orchestra played a boisterous overture.

Everyone had his own program.

The lanterns were dimmed. The curtains slowly parted. The full moon shone down. It was time to begin.

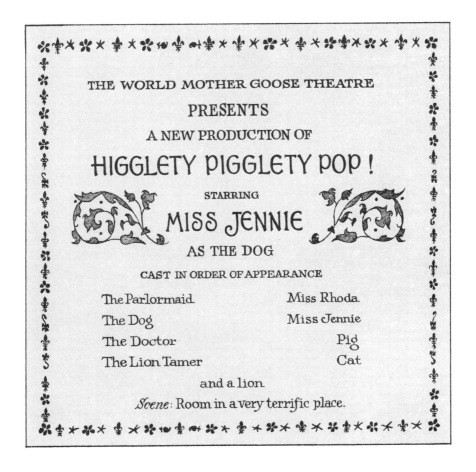

THE WORLD MOTHER GOOSE THEATRE

PRESENTS

A NEW PRODUCTION OF

HIGGLETY PIGGLETY POP !

STARRING

MISS JENNIE

AS THE DOG

CAST IN ORDER OF APPEARANCE

The Parlormaid	Miss Rhoda
The Dog	Miss Jennie
The Doctor	Pig
The Lion Tamer	Cat

and a lion

Scene: Room in a very terrific place.

Epilogue

Now Jennie has everything. She is the finest leading lady The World Mother Goose Theatre ever had. Jennie is a star. She performs every day and twice on Saturday. She is content.

Once Jennie sent her old master a letter. This is what it said:

Hello,

As you probably noticed, I went away forever. I am very experienced now and very famous. I am even a star. Every day I eat a mop, twice on Saturday. It is made of salami and that is my favorite. I get plenty to drink too, so don't worry. I can't tell you how to get to the Castle Yonder because I don't know where it is. But if you ever come this way, look for me.

                                                              Jennie